also by Brooks Hansen:

Boone (co-authored with Nick Davis)

The Chess Garden

Perlman's Ordeal

Caesar's Antlers

The Monsters of St. Helena

The Brotherhood of Joseph

John the Baptizer

Asmodeus: the Legend of Margrét and the Dragon

BEASTIE:
Lord of the Lamp Post

a recollection
(with drawings)
by

Brooks Hansen

STAR PINE

Cover art and design by Brooks Hansen
Interior art by Brooks Hansen
Printed and bound in the United States of America
Second edition
978-0-9973979-4-9

To anyone who'll play

Contents

Lord of the Lamp Post

With perfect poise the bronze await,
while passers gaze, and painters paint,
while sticky-fingered babies
muck their ears and noses.
All throughout the park they stay
as nannies read and children play.
With dignity and no complaint
the statues hold their poses.

Even when the sun descends
and all the paths begin to clear,
when lamps alight to welcome night,
no pigeon is so impolite
as to suppose that anyone is here.
Not while the Beastie sleeps.

It's only when the moon eludes the cloud-bank,
and every peering bedroom light goes dim,
when darkness looms in quiet rooms,
and closets stand like mummy's tombs,
and the last child's dream is finally entered in,
that's when the shadow slips out from its dungeon,
and tumbles down to fetch itself a drink,
to forage in the trees for midnight luncheon,
and just like that make chiseled eyelids blink,

and fingers twitch, and noses itch
and round bronze shoulders sink.
From meer to lake, they'll all awake
from bridle path,
       to reservoir,
          to rink…

…shall Alice and her friends
descend the toadstool,
the duck look down
and Andersen stand up,
shall statesmen turn
their sculpted heads,
crack free their heels,
tramp flower beds,
while noted busts from
pedestals un-cup.

But the only one who'll ever get to see them
is the only one who ever lets them see:
They're not alone.
There's flesh and bone.
There's pointy ears,
and fingernails, and teeth.
There is the Beastie,
shaggy Beastie,
Lord of the Lamp Post!

So the siblings in the garden quit the fountain,
set down their bowls to drink the evening air.
The seraphim stretch out their wings,
and statesmen state some stately things.
The pilgrim prays.
The muses wash their hair.

The animal band that twirls around the zoo clock
will all break free and flee the entry arch.
Some head down to the merry-go-round
to watch the soldiers march,
while Alice lounges on the lawns,
eating apples made of bronze,
and cherubs cross the bridge in each direction,
while horses graze, and lizards laze,
while kings attack the meadow haze,
and ugly ducklings pity their reflection.
And they converse and they digress.
They plot, they scheme, and they confess,
though to what we can but guess...

...as the only one who ever really hears them
is the only one who ever lets them hear:
his moon-ward howl, his stomach growl,
his gnaw, his paw, his grunt, his scratch, his cheer.
All hail the Beastie,
shaggy Beastie,
Lord of the Lamp Post!

So for the while the poets float on rowboats.
The door-mouse roars, and governors patrol.
The busts burst out in evening song.
The Indian hunter joins along.
The falcon flies. The husky digs a hole.

But just as every day
will soon enough give way to night,
so must darkness yield to light;
they all can see it creep up from the east.
The bronze cock crows,
the whole park knows it's time –
for hero, deity, and beast.

They choose the quickest paths back to their places.
They reckon thoughts to conjure faces.
The pilgrim flares his boots and stands his gun.
Jaggiello climbs up to his mount.
The angel crowns the water fount.
Each one of them to right where it begun:

Alice to her toadstool; the kitten to her lap;
Hans Christian sets his storybook on knee.
He opens to the page again,
the one that locks his cage again.
The duckling lifts his bill so he can see.

By then the Beastie's safe inside,
upon a slab that's three feet wide,
exhausted from his night and turning in.
The lamp posts snuff, that was enough.
The sun's returned. Its first rays scissor in.

And when they touch Tecumseh's cheek,
that's when the last should steal its peek,
as after that they stiffen and they stay.
Their light recedes to other needs
To summon anyone who reads,
        or strolls,
           or paints,
              …or anyone who'll play.

                      –   *Anonymous*

Chapter One:
the tub

One spring when I was nine and my sister
Molly was twelve, our parents went away on a trip
together, just the two of them, to France. They had
never asked for such a thing before, so neither my
sister nor I felt we could object. They said they'd
only be gone a week.

My mother arranged for two babysitters to take
care of us. The younger and more appealing was
Claire. Claire was either in college or graduate
school, I'm not sure, but she had shiny, light brown
hair, a knack for drawing very goofy, very detailed

 characters almost as
quickly as you could
describe them, and she
made Shepherd's Pie for
dinner. I liked Claire a lot.
Also, there was a song on

the radio at that time called "Claire," which may have had something to do with it.

The other sitter was to be Mrs. Guildenweiser, the old lady who lived in the apartment next door, and who owned a very poorly behaved black poodle named Lara, who leapt and barked from behind her door any time she heard the elevator. Mrs. Guildenweiser took care of me in the afternoons sometimes, and she wasn't so bad. She had a way of making tuna fish sandwiches, with the toast kept separate from the tuna, and buttered, that was mysteriously delicious. But for reasons I've already indicated, she was no Claire, and my mother had made clear that Claire was to be the real babysitter. Claire would be picking us up from school and spending the night.

The first day was fine, a Monday. My parents said good bye to us under the awning, then they climbed in a cab with their suitcases and headed off to the airport. Molly and I climbed onto a bus with our backpacks and went off to school – two different schools actually, one for boys, one for girls, and just two blocks apart.

I was in fourth grade, and my teacher that year was Mr. Ryan, who was by far my favorite teacher up to then. He had served in Korea, in the Navy, but he was a little bit egg-shaped now. He wore his belt high and in the middle. His button-down shirts tended to be short-sleeved. He had black horn-rimmed glasses and he slicked back his hair like Elvis Presley, though his nose was pointier, and he had a double chin. But none of that mattered because he was also, hands-down, the best storyteller I had ever heard – the funniest and wisest and the most entertaining – and he seemed to be fond of me too. When my mother first told him that she and my dad would be gone that week, Mr. Ryan just gave me a pat on the shoulder. "We'll hold the fort," he said, and that seemed to me to be a pretty good way of looking at it.

Softball season had begun. I was on coach Willie's Blue Team. I played shortstop that day, as I tended to, and got a couple hits, all of which I shared with Claire when she came to pick me up that afternoon, but only because she asked. We took the bus back down along the park, and I stuck to my usual routine when we got home. I did my homework first thing. I staged a brief siege with my fort and soldiers, then as soon as Molly got home we all had dinner together – shepherd's pie and apple pie with ice cream (because you can't have too much pie, Claire said). We drew pictures and watched TV until 8:30. I slept in Molly's room. We pulled the trundle out from under her bed.

§

The second day was when the trouble started. School was more or less the same. Mr. Ryan told us the story of the Trojan Horse. One of the seventh graders got his nostril torn in an eraser fight, and the Blue team won. I played shortstop again and hit a triple, but the real hi-light was coach Willie teaching us all the Blue Team Fight Song. We helped him write it – or it seemed like that, anyway – and we agreed we would sing it together on the way to every game.

It went like this:

> Take off your shoes and stockings,
> And let your feet hang bare.
> We are the Blue Team of St. David's,
> Touch us if you dare.
>
> We carry knives and pistols
> And little bullets too.
> And if you dare to touch us,
> We'll split you right in two.
>
> Give a yell!
> Give a yell!
> Give a good substantial yell!
> And when we yell we yell like hell
> And this is what we yell:
>
> Mary had a little lamb
> Little lamb, little lamb
> Mary had a little lamb
> Whose fleece was white as snow.

11

BEASTIE

Hurrah for Mary!
Hurrah for the lamb!
Hurrah for the Blue Team,
Who doesn't give a
Nah nah-nah nah nah!

It was a good song, and I was looking forward to sharing it with Claire at the end of the day because I was pretty sure she was going to like it too, even if it was a little violent in parts. But when the final bell rang and I made my way down the main stairs to meet her, I could tell even before I reached the first landing that Claire hadn't come to pick me up. I heard Lara barking, and probably leaping at someone and licking them and sniffing them, and I knew that Mrs. Guildenweiser had come instead.

Mrs. Guildenweiser (whose name was not as complicated as it looked; it was pronounced 'golden-visor') was, as I mentioned, much older than Claire. And shorter. She was my height, in fact, about four and a half feet tall on account of a severe hunchback, and her face was shaped a lot like a witch's. Her hair was grey at the roots and a chalky red on top. Her eyebrows were pencil-thin, and pencil-drawn, and her expression was droll. She had seen a lot in her life, my mother said. She had fled Hungary when she was younger.

Her manner that afternoon was typically off-hand. Claire was sick, she said. Nothing serious. "A bad piece of fish," she guessed. She said my mother and father were aware. She had spoken to them already, and assured them that everything was fine, she would take care of us until Claire had recovered.

"You don't want to spoil their trip," she said, and I had to agree. I didn't want that.

Lara wasn't allowed on the bus, so we had to walk home, and stop at the grocery store on the way. We bought a lot of things I didn't like the looks of – generic brands and strange soaps in strange bottles – and I had to carry them home, even though I was carrying my book bag as well.

BEASTIE

When we finally got back to the apartment, Lara barged in ahead of us and started sniffing in all the corners and smacking her very stiff tail against the furniture. Mrs. Guildenweiser offered to make a tuna sandwich, but I said no. I got myself a glass of milk, stirred in some Quick, and went to my room to count my mitts.

I had nine, which was a point of pride but also of shame, since nine mitts was probably seven more than anyone should need. On the other hand, I took very good care of them, oiling them and breaking them in, keeping them all loose and in use. I had one for every position: a first baseman's mitt, though I almost never played first base; an outfielder's glove, which was very large and loose and raggedy on the inside, but had always served me well; a pitcher's mitt, or what I liked to think of as a pitcher's mitt, which had been an excellent glove in its day, up until I tried to adjust its pocket by leaving it under the tire of the Volkswagen overnight; it had been spackled with road-tar ever since. An infielder by trade, I had several smaller gloves – last year's (good pocket, loose and deep); the one from the year before that, which was too small; and then my current gamer, of course, the one I carried to and from school in my book bag, and without doubt the best work I'd ever done.

Probably the most *distinctive* of my mitts, however, was the catcher's mitt, the roundest and thickest in the collection, and which for that reason had required the most work breaking in. The strange thing was, I couldn't seem to find it that afternoon. It wasn't in the basket. It wasn't in the bin. It wasn't under my bed. It wasn't anywhere.

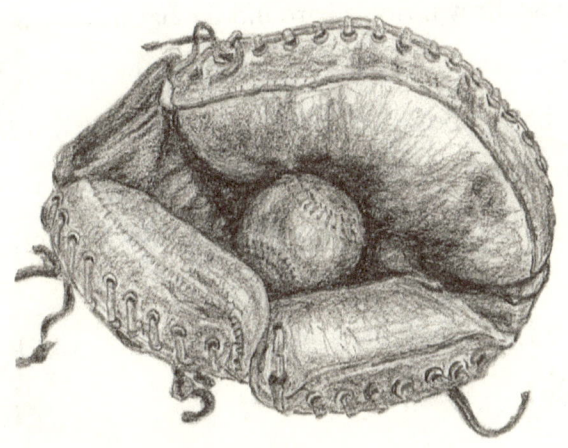

BEASTIE

I was standing up on my desk chair, searching the high shelves in my closet when my sister's voice came screeching down from the end of the hall.

"Eeeeeiiew! Eeiw, eeiew, eiew. Grossss!"

I hadn't even known Molly was home.

"Gro-oooosssss!"

Lara started barking, and Mrs. Guildenweiser came waddling after as fast as she could. I met them at the door of the bathroom, which is where Molly was, leaning back against the sink on one foot, and scowling at the tub. We all looked in.

There was nothing *inside* the tub exactly, but Molly was right, this was a little gross. There was a smudgy brown ring all around the basin, strewn with coarse black hairs. Grosser still, the scrub-brush was upside-down against the wall, its bristles all tangled with thick black hair and soap.

"Tsk, tsk, tsk," clucked Mrs. Guildenweiser.

Lara barked.

"Did you give her a bath in the tub?" asked Molly.

Mrs. Guildenweiser scoffed no. "Look at it." As she waved at the tub-sides, her bracelets jangled, it was true. This really didn't look like Lara's hair. It was straight and thick, like bristles. Mrs. Guildenweiser rolled herself a handful of toilet paper and used it to swipe up the soapy black clump that was clogging the drain. All the bracelets slid down her skinny wrinkled wrist and back up to her elbow as she lifted the filthy gob to her nose.

"Beastie, Beastie, Beastie." She gently shook her head and opened the cabinet below the sink to get a sponge and some cleanser.

"What's Beastie?" I asked.

"Nothing," said Molly. "There isn't any Beastie. It's Lara."

Mrs. Guildenweiser just shrugged and started the tap, and that's when I saw: there on the bath mat was the muddy print of what looked like a very long, very . . . well, *beastly*, foot. Before I could get a good look at it, though, Molly kicked at the mat – intentionally. Just like that, the print was gone, as was all the dirt on the tub-sides now, and the hair, vanishing in swirls beneath Mrs. Guildenweiser's sponge, and sudsing down the drain.

§

Kind of oddly, it seemed to me, nothing more was said about the tub at dinner, thanks mostly to Molly's and Mrs. Guildenweiser's both being very stubborn. They clinked their plates and chewed – chicken and wax beans. Mrs. Guildenweiser didn't eat at all, just sat with us and tapped her fingers patiently, humming but making no sound. When we were done, Molly and I watched TV for an hour and half, in silence. Three shows.

Finally, I couldn't stand it anymore. During one of the commercials, I went to the kitchen to get a drink. Mrs. Guildenweiser was sitting at the table by the window, having tea and toast and looking out at the street.

"So what's Beastie?" I asked.

She replied with a sniff and smile meant to reassure. "Oh, he's nothing to worry about." She waved her hand, her bracelets clinked. "He prefers the park."

"Then what was he doing here?"

"Washing, I suppose." She shrugged. "Spring cleaning. Everyone's entitled." She lifted the tea-cup to her mouth and murmured inside, "and high time, too."

She seemed awfully casual about the whole thing. I couldn't help thinking it was because this wasn't really *her* home.

"Do we know he's gone?"

"Oh, yes, I'm sure," she said. "But we could check."

I agreed, it probably made sense to check, and for once I was glad that Lara was there. The three of us went through the whole apartment, room by room, cupboard by cupboard, chest by chest. We checked the living room. The dining room. The front hall closets.

BEASTIE

Molly could tell what we were doing. She called out from her throne of pillows in front of the TV, "There's no such *thi-ing.*"

But we went on. We checked the bathrooms, the bedrooms, the bedroom closets, my parents' room as well.

"She's *ly-ing!*" called Molly, now from her and my bathroom, brushing her teeth. "Mrs. Guildenweiser is lying!"

But we went ahead and checked the locks on all the doors and windows. We did a thorough job, and by the time we were done I was convinced that if there was a beast who'd come to take a bath in our tub, at least it was no longer *in* the apartment. Still, just to be safe, I wore my Jets helmet to bed that night, which once again I spent in Molly's room.

"It isn't true," said Molly, setting up her pillows. "You know that. It was Lara, which is still really gross."

I nodded. I wanted to believe her, but –

"Oh, look at you," Mrs. Guildenweiser hooted

as she came in to say good night, Lara trotting in behind her, her stiff tail thumping Molly's bedpost. She started licking my face guard.

"Why do you wear that contraption on your head?" asked Mrs. Guildenweiser. "You can't sleep in that."

"Cold," I said.

"He's not going to come and eat you. You're much too big and bony, and I told you, he prefers the park at night."

"You shouldn't be saying that," said Molly. "You're scaring him."

Mrs. Guildenweiser doubted that. "Am I scaring you?"

No, I shook my head.

"No, because there's nothing to be scared of," she said. "He came. He took a bath. He left. Could be much worse."

She patted my helmet, Lara gave it one more lick, then the two of them left. *Thwack-thwack.*

My sister and I didn't talk much after that. I

convinced her to keep the light on in the bathroom. "But she's still lying," is all she felt it necessary to say, for the eighteenth time. She read briefly – Madeleine L'Engle, then fell asleep right away, leaving me awake and alone to watch the curtains billow, and to listen to the whooshing trees outside.

Something could easily have come in, if it wanted. I tried to think of our parents and where they were. Was it morning there yet? Did they have bicycles? But then the curtains would catch my eye again, and my mind would return: What was to stop it? Where else had it gone?

…And where in the world was my catcher's mitt?

Chapter Two:
the library

I didn't mention Beastie to anyone at school on Wednesday – not my friends John or Rob or Anthony, or even Mr. Ryan. I wished I could have said something, but Mrs. Guildenweiser had made it clear over breakfast: The Beastie wasn't something you should talk about with others, in particular those who didn't already know.

She chose a very strange way of putting it, though.

"It's like this coffee," she said, tapping her cup. "You have tasted coffee?"

I nodded, I had. Out of curiosity once.

"Did you like it?"

I shook my head, no. It tasted like dirt.

"But you see," said Mrs.

Guildenweiser. "One day you'll wake up, and you will look out the window, and you will think to yourself, 'I would like a cup of coffee today. A cup of coffee sounds like the most delicious thing in the world to me!' And you will drink the coffee, and it will be exactly what you wanted." To demonstrate the point, she treated herself to a slow, trembling sip. "It's the same with the Beastie. When a person is ready to see him, he will see him. Until then —" She put her finger to her lips. "It's best for everyone — best for Beastie, too."

I wasn't sure I entirely agreed with her reasoning — and I also wondered why anyone should care what was best for *Beastie* — but I could sense there was wisdom in keeping the knowledge to myself.

And the truth was, when I finally did get to school and saw all my friends out front, whacking each other with their book-bags, it didn't take long for the thought to slip away — a safe distance. Mr. Ryan spoke to us about the Spartans in class. At recess, we played Kill the Carrier on the deck, and then at lunch Alec Cushman blew his nose and missed his napkin.

School proved an able distraction, that is to say, and as the day drew on, it even began to seem silly, the idea – a beast living in the park. Molly was right. That had been Lara's hair in the tub – obviously – and Mrs. Guildenweiser was just being Mrs. Guildenweiser.

Then came sports. We all changed into our sneakers and gym clothes and made our way across the street to the park, but the moment we passed through the dark stone entrance, I could feel something was different. Something had changed. Even as we all joined in singing the Blue Team Fight Song, I could sense it – as if there were eyes in all the tree-limbs and bushes, peering out at us and wishing we would go. It felt like we were invading someone else's home.

We went out to the softball diamonds, the ones next to the turtle pond and the castle that seemed to grow from the rock – Belvedere. But even there, with nothing but the wide blue sky spanning above, I still felt like an intruder. It wasn't until the game actually started that I was able to relax at all. In the bottom of the third inning, Ken Kennerly hit a grounder just under Andy McGillicuddy's glove – Andy was playing third – but I managed to lunge and catch it in the webbing. I turned and from my knees threw to first base, barely nipping Ken, who was by no means slow.

"The garbage man!" called Mr. Blindman, who was another one of the coaches. He meant because I picked up everything. "Nice play!"

Nice glove, I thought, and gave it a punch.

As soon as the game was over and we started back for school, I felt that same uneasiness again. We passed by a pair of squirrels scrambling up a tree trunk, then a covey of pigeons snacking on the path. I had always suspected they knew something, with their twitching heads and nervous eyes – some secret they were keeping. Finally now I knew what it was.

I met Molly after school at the bus stop and we rode home together so that Mrs. Guildenweiser wouldn't have to make the walk. We sat all the way in the back on the hot seats, and as the bus wheezed along from stop to stop, I kept looking out the window at the low stone wall that ran alongside the park – the whole way around, except for the little entrances punched here and there. It had never

27

occurred to me before, why the park should need such a dark and constant barrier.

"I asked Mrs. Fitzgerald," said Molly, who could tell what I was thinking. "She said the same thing. She said it was just a legend."

I didn't care what Mrs. Fitzgerald said. I didn't know who Mrs. Fitzgerald was, and I didn't think Molly should be asking other people about the Beastie anyway.

We got off at our usual stop near the hot dog wagon. Sometimes with my mother, I would get a hot dog before going home, but I wasn't hungry that day, and it looked like the hot dog man was heading in early. Amal was his name.

As Molly and I stood waiting for the light to change, Amal pulled the hot dog bin from its slot and dumped it into the nearest grate, all the dogs and water together. They splashed and hissed as the subterranean gutter swallowed them up and carried them away to what I assumed was some great reservoir beneath the park.

Made sense, I thought. Amal was in on it too.

Molly grabbed my hand; she'd seen enough. "Come on. I'll prove it to you."

We crossed the street, then the cross-street, which meant we weren't going home. She was taking me to the neighborhood library.

It wasn't a very big library, this one. It was more like a small mansion made of gray-white stone, and it was peaceful inside, and creaky and quiet like church. The surfaces were all soft marble or burnished wood, and no one ever spoke above a whisper.

It was fairly late in the day, so there weren't many people there – a few old men in the front room, thumbing through map books and dictionaries. Molly led me straight to the card catalogue and pulled out a long skinny drawer, "Ba - Bu." She seemed to know exactly where to go and what to do. She flipped through the cards and stopped in the middle.

"There," she whispered, "P-786."

She kept repeating this to herself as she took my hand and led me back to the main hall and up a curving marble staircase.

The second floor was partly lined with glass cases and statues, but through a wooden door was another large room facing the street. There were leather chairs and desks with lamps, and a rack of magazines and newspapers, but the only other person there was a slender little man reading a foreign newspaper. He had thin golden hair and narrow shoulders with wide lapels and a very large knot in his tie. His face was spindly but handsome. In fact, I recognized him. He interviewed people on TV.

Molly, undistracted and still determined, crossed straight to the far side of the room, eyeing the shelves along the walls and silently mouthing the number P-786.

"Here," she whispered. She pulled out a tall slim book. It had a canvassy cover with a very dark image on it – of a lit lamp post at night. That was all, except it looked like there was something perched on top of the lamp post, only the light was so bright and the dark was so dark, you could barely make out the shape. There might have been a low-swinging arm, and also a pair of pointy black ears on the head.

More clear was the title:

BEASTIE:
Lord of the Lamp Post

Molly opened the book carefully. The pages were yellow and flaky, and there weren't very many of them – for a book. Or many words either. All it was was a poem.

Molly started reading it to herself silently – she didn't want to bother the man with the newspaper. I tried to follow along, but I didn't read as quickly as my sister, especially at an angle. I really only understood bits and pieces until Molly turned to the second page. I saw the word because she pointed to it: "Beastie," it said, "the shaggy beastie." I saw the

31

words "pointy ears" as well, and "finger nails" and "teeth."

"See," whispered Molly. "It's just a poem."

At this, the man reading the foreign newspaper, the one from TV, gently cleared his throat.

"Sorry," said Molly, hushing herself, but the man shook his head. He didn't mean to scold us. He'd meant to get our attention.

"What are you reading?" he asked, sounding very interested, and patient, and intelligent.

"Nothing," said Molly. "It's just a poem."

"What's it about?" He folded his paper neatly.

"Nothing," said Molly.

"Hm," he smiled and stood. "Sounds dull." He was very small and slender, as it turned out, but his suit was a perfect little fit.

"Perhaps you'd find this book more interesting."

He tapped the shelf beside him. Or it wasn't a shelf exactly. It was the brace *between* the shelves, only someone – I assume it was he – had slid aside the cover screen to reveal a hidden compartment. It was twice the height of the other shelves, but much more narrow, just wide enough for one secret book, and we probably couldn't have read the spine, it was pushed so deep into the shadow, except that the letters were very large, very few, and embossed in gold:

B

S

T

Y

The man from TV looked back at us – at me actually – and winked. Then he returned the paper to its rack and excused himself, whisper-whistling out the door and into the hall.

Molly seemed to have found all this more annoying than strange, but there was still no question we had to go look. As soon as we could hear the little man's heels start clicking down the marble stairs, we hustled over to the shelf. The BSTY book was so heavy, it took the two of us together to pull it out and heave it down. Molly collapsed into the leather chair, and the book flounced open on her lap.

It was actually more like an album, filled with clippings and letters and little drawings, all glued in, or slid in. And they were all extremely old and fragile-looking, so Molly tried to be gentle. She let the pages flip to where they wanted, and they stopped near the middle, at a handwritten letter – four leaves on facing pages, bearing a very clear and enviable cursive.

Molly's lips began to move.

"Out loud," I said.

No one was there now, so she obliged. I came round behind her so I could follow along and make sure as I listened.

"'Your honour'," she began:

Please accept my apology that it should have taken these three months for my reply. My only excuse is an abhorrence for the events at question, as they did mar and steal from me what should otherwise have been my most precious memory, of the blessed night that I and Mrs. T_____ were wed.

But to the end which you so wisely and courageously propose, let the present document testify the truth of what I know, concerning what took place the evening of August 22, 1885.

"All right, all right," said Molly. "So that just means he's going to tell us now."

That was pretty much what I'd figured, but I was grateful for the translation. She continued.

It bears reminding that this was only two days after the disappearance of the Vandeweghe children. The city was, I think it safe to say, in a state if greater-than-unusual anxiety. The Times had run its piece. The search was under way. We as yet knew nothing of little Kitty's somnambulism, or of the uncle's gambling debts. Nonetheless, my wife's family, of sturdy

Swedish stock, had decided that our nuptials should proceed as planned; this, despite the fact that they were to be held just one block from the Vandeweghe mansion, and just three blocks from the siblings' favorite —and at that point in time, most infamous — playground.

"Got it?" asked Molly.

"Some kids were missing, so everyone was nervous, but this guy went ahead with his wedding anyway."

"And I get the feeling they were rich." She continued.

_The choice had seemed vindicated. The ceremony proceeded without event; likewise, the celebration afterward, held in the ballroom at the P____ Hotel._

_Following this, it had been arranged that Mrs. T____ and I should take, as our first conjugal journey together, a carriage ride through the southern loop of Central Park._

"You know where they are?" asked Molly.

"Near the zoo?" I said. "And why did people

write like this?"

"No idea," said Molly, and she continued.

> *It was the night of the new moon, and I
> shouldn't have to tell you that, especially back
> then, that region of the park was very poorly lit,
> as result of which I could feel my wife's
> nervousness almost from the moment we entered
> in, expressed most acutely in the grip with
> which she held my hand. I knew that she was
> thinking of the missing children, and of the
> playground, as I myself was thinking of them.
> As was the coachman, I suspect.*
>
> *Stranger still, it even seemed that our
> unease was beginning to infect the hale and
> hardy Clydesdale pulling our carriage. His
> disturbance first registered as sniffs and snorts,
> which wouldn't have been so remarkable, except
> that these gave the distinct impression that he
> had detected something particular in the air,
> some foul scent of which the rest of us were as
> yet unaware.*
>
> *The coachman did his best to quiet him.
> Flick-flick, he scolded with his whip, but the
> poor workhorse only seemed to grow more
> agitated the further along the path we ventured,
> jerking and jostling the carriage to such an*

extent, the implication was now unavoidable,
that lurking somewhere in the fog that had
enveloped us was a menace of some kind, a
dark presence at which even this great steed felt
a clearly mortal threat.

This struggle continued, between whip and
instinct, until we reached the foot of the reflect-
ing bridge, at which point the horse outright
refused to proceed another step.

"Apologies, apologies," the coachman turned
to reassure, but by now my bride's alarm was
well beyond such consolation. She was upset not
just by the eerie sense that we were being
followed – or stalked –but also by the vicious
beating that the coachman was now visiting
upon the hide of his loyal horse and livelihood.

*"Make him stop," she cried, and I was on
the verge of doing so, of physically collaring the
man, when suddenly I smelt it too — a terrible,
and what I can only describe as a very <u>beastly</u>,
stench.*

"We should stop," said Molly. "This is dumb."

"No," I said. I didn't think this was dumb at all.
"Hurry. From there," I pointed, and she continued
reluctantly.

*And now the horse reared up and gave out such a
terrified and wide-eyed shriek, I suspect I shall
be hearing its echo until my dying day. I scanned
the shadows up ahead, and my eye was drawn to
the nearest light, where all at once I saw it: Atop
the lamp post at the far end of the bridge, there
perched what looked at first like a kind of
gargoyle, but that unlike a gargoyle, it was
covered with a dense and ragged coat of —*

Molly stopped again for some reason. I elbowed her
to keep going, but then I looked up to see a woman
standing at the door. She was tall and wide-hipped,
with a long pale face, and a pair of reading glasses

hanging from a chain around her neck.

"Oh." She seemed surprised to have found anyone there. "I'm sorry. The library is closing now."

We could hear it, too, the sound of closing books and all the old readers shuffling out across the marble floor downstairs. Molly nodded, and the album thumped shut on her lap.

The librarian noticed, and I could tell from the expression on her face – or really, the deliberate lack of any expression – she knew very well which book that was. Her eye passed over the secret compartment with an equal, and equally telling, absence of concern. "Where did you find that?"

"Nowhere," said Molly. "It was here on the chair." (And why my sister felt it necessary to protect the man from TV, I had no idea. But I was glad she did.)

"Oh," said the librarian again. Abruptly, then, she started straight toward us. She walked right up to Molly, leaned down and took the book directly from her lap. It was a little frightening, but then she didn't seem to know quite what to do. She just stood there a moment – her fingers clasped so tightly to the cover, I could see the veins and tendons dancing across the backs of her hands – and I understood that whatever finally happened to Mr. T-blank and his new bride (or to little Kitty Vandeweghe and her brother, for that matter) was likely lost to me forever.

"I'm afraid you have to go," she said.

Molly didn't protest. She took my hand and tugged me away, all the way down the spiral marble stairs, through the entry and out onto the street again.

Chapter Three:
the tunnel

Molly did her best to explain away Mr. T-blank's letter.

"That doesn't prove anything," she said as we walked home, and we were walking very quickly now. "It proves it's a story. It proves it's something people once believed in, or thought they saw. But it's still just a *legend*. Plus, the letter said 1885. Animals don't live that long."

I appreciated her effort, and it was enough to get me through dinner. After dessert, Claire called to tell us she was feeling better.

"Are you coming?" I asked, as soon as it was my turn.

"I don't think so," she said, and her nose did sound stuffed. "I don't want to get you sick too. Do you forgive me?"

Of course I forgave her. Still I wished she were here, because I was pretty sure none of this would have happened if she had been, or at least she'd have been much more reassuring than either Mrs. Guildenweiser or Molly. As it was, and as bedtime began to loom, I could feel myself starting to have doubts again. In the first place, it simply wasn't true that animals didn't live that long, since 1885. Tortoises easily lived that long, and who said Beastie was an animal anyway? Or couldn't have off-spring?

After brushing my teeth, I decided to try to find my catcher's mitt again, just in case whoever took it might have put it back. But it still wasn't there, and now I couldn't find my baseball either – the older one, the deep green-brown one, even though I could have sworn I'd seen it yesterday. I started pulling all the sticks and bats from the tall bin when

BEASTIE

I was suddenly stopped short by a sound. It was coming from outside. Someone was laughing. I turned to the window and looked.

It was a warm breezy night, and clear. The street below was lit all the way along for the stray passing cars, as were the buildings on the far side of the park, all standing in their places like soldiers in glowing uniforms. The park lay mostly black between them, the darkest thing there was, except for tiny lamp posts all throughout – like lights in a giant Christmas tree, each one shedding a little glowing puddle, just large enough to see: there was the bridge you had to cross to get to the fields; there was the bench where I'd sat when I was sick that time; there, the garbage can.

And just as I was looking at it, a shadow passed, fast as a bird but bigger. Then came the giggling again, and hushing– *"Sh-sh-sh. Sh-sh-sh"*– and it was gone, swallowed in the darkness and hiss of blowing leaves.

But who could be in the park at this time of

night? I wondered. And then I thought, Who else?

I closed the window. I pulled the shade. I went and got a flashlight from my drawer, and crawled all the way back to the far corner of my bed. It took a long time to get to sleep that night, with my shoulders wedged against the walls, and my pillow wrapped around my ears, trying with all my might not to think about the shadow down below, swinging from post to post.

§

I was tired the following day. I almost fell asleep in class, which Mr. Ryan must have seen. He found me later at recess, which we had to have indoors that day, in the small gym, because it was raining outside.

"Are you all right there?" he asked. "You seem a little out of sorts."

I, who was sitting out this round of Kill the Carrier, admitted it with a nod.

"When are your parents due?"

"Friday."

Mr. Ryan gave a rock on his heels and turned his attention back to the game. "Easy there, Anthony. Easy." (Anthony was tackling Douglas Knepper by the sleeve.)

"Are legends true?" I asked, out of what must have seemed to be the blue.

Mr. Ryan looked down. "What's that?" He cupped his ear as more of the boys stampeded by.

"I just don't understand," I said, waiting. "Are legends true or not?"

Mr. Ryan took a moment to think about it. He crossed his arms and rubbed his chin and looked up at the ceiling of the gym. "Well, I guess that depends on the legend. Which one were you thinking of?"

"…Robin Hood?" I suggested.

"Robin Hood? Oh, of course. Earl of Huntington." He leaned down close so only I would hear, and assumed his thickest oldest English accent:

> 'Lyeth and listen, gentleman,
>   that be of freebore blood.
> I shall you tell of a good yeman,
>   whose name was Robin Hood!'

He stopped himself, seeming to realize this wasn't really helping. "Now, did he actually split the arrow? That I can't promise you."

I understood. "What about King Arthur?"

"Oh, of course. Son of Luther Pendragon."
Mr. Ryan particularly liked the name 'Luther
Pendragon', and took every opportunity to say it,
which is part of the reason I'd picked it. "Luther
Pendragon-son! He most certainly existed, but
again, did he pull the sword from the stone? I think
it's possible there may have been some
embellishments along the way."

Mr. Ryan could see that his answer still wasn't
doing the trick, so he paused another moment to
think.

"I guess what it boils down to," he finally said,
"is that if something is called a 'legend', that means
there must be something true in it, but that there's
also probably something false, and it's our job to
figure out which is which."

I nodded, trying not to show my disappoint-
ment. This was pretty much what I'd thought.

§

The rain let up briefly after lunch, which I actually wished it hadn't, because it meant we all had to go out to the park and I wouldn't have minded staying in the gym that day. But after final period, we all put on our sneakers and sweats and hooded gray sweatshirts and crossed the street, which was still slick and shiny from the rain.

Even in the park, the water was still rivering along the gutters, and cascading down the drain grates to join the rushing waters underneath. We sang the Blue Team fight song, which briefly lifted my spirits, but I could still feel that lump in my throat. I tried consoling myself with what Mr. Ryan had said: there was probably something false about the Beastie – and clearly the most likely thing to be false was that he really existed, or still existed. Probably he was just something that people liked to tease other people about, despite the look in all the pigeons' eyes, and the squirrels'.

When we finally got out to the fields, the baseball diamond was all mud and puddles; the batter's box was an eight-shaped pool. We had to go all the way to the far side before we found a diamond we could play on, nearest the turtle pond. There was a group of tourists out on the terrace of the Castle, their cameras all shuttering and rewinding while the sky was clear. They didn't seem to know. How could so many people not know something that was true?

As the Blue Team took the field, the clouds were pulling over again like a giant gray mattress, and the first drops of rain were falling. The other team, the Reds, made three quick outs, all on pop-ups, then as I was coming off the field, Christopher Nelson asked if he could borrow my mitt; he'd forgotten his. I said yes, even though Christopher Nelson wasn't much of a player and he used to smell a little like pee in kindergarten, but I had to let him have my mitt. He'd asked.

The drops were growing heavier now, and harder. I led off, and mostly because of the rain, swung at the first pitch. Fly ball to left, and fairly deep. It was headed straight for Christopher Nelson, in fact, who instantly began to stagger and panic. But just as the ball reached its apex, the sky cracked and shuddered. The tourists on the castle terrace gasped, then down came a sudden gush of rain, so fast it practically hit the ground before the ball. Christopher Nelson covered his head with my glove and ran. All the Reds did. Then the Blues. We gathered under the trees behind the backstop first, and coach Willie led the charge to the nearest foot bridge – the tunnel underneath, that is.

We were all soaked by the time we got there, but we still had to wait, all huddled together in the little dank tunnel. The water was coming down in billowing sheets now; we could hardly see the castle. I got my mitt back, then joined John and Anthony and Rob. Rob was entertaining us with monkey faces, and John started hooting.

Hoo-hoo. Hoo-hoo.

The sound of it echoed against the arched brick, and now a few others joined in –Anthony and

51

Andy McGillicuddy, and Coach Willie didn't
bother to stop us. There wasn't much else to do
while we were there, and no strangers who'd be
bothered, so suddenly we all started hooting. Me
too, and with all of us together, it sounded like a
giant flock of owls trapped inside a cave, or owls
and monkeys, hooting and *eee-eeeking* and *aaa-
aaaaking,* trying to drown out the rain, when all of
the sudden John started shushing everyone.

"*Sh, sh, sh!* Listen! Listen."

And one by one, hoot by hoot, we did go quiet,
because John was right. There was a strange sort of
grunting, snorting sound coming from the water
drain. The moment I heard it I knew. Even with the
water rushing underneath, it was still clear, as if the
current were carrying the echo like a boat.

"What *is* that?" asked John

"Sounds like someone snoring," said Rob, and
the others nodded – a deep, clicking, snarling snore,
like the kind that my father made when he was
joking.

"Hey, wake up," said Michael Dooley, trying to be funny. Michael Dooley was probably my least favorite classmates because he liked to act much tougher than he was and his nose was always running. "Wake up, wake up!" He started stomping on the grate with his sneakers, but thankfully coach Willie pulled him back

"Let him be, let him sleep."

"He sounds big," said John.

And close, I thought. The sound was all around us now, and I could picture him, a large dark shadow, sleeping in a cavern, while the water rushed by just beneath the lip of his limestone bed. Or concrete. Or shimmering mica schist.

Suddenly there came a much louder snort from the drain, and a shift. He was stirring awake, and all of us jumped back – Coach Willie, included. He stuck his hand out into the rain. It was still coming down, but not as hard as before.

"This may be as good as it gets," he said. "Let's make a run for it."

BEASTIE

None of us objected. We all put our mitts on our heads, those of us who remembered to bring our mitts, and ran yelling out into the rain, away from whoever that was, or whatever that was, trying to sleep in the bowels of the park.

Chapter Four:
the trooper

That afternoon, Molly and I took the bus home together again. The sky had cleared. The sun was even coming out. People were streaming into the park, but I sat on the far side of the bus. I didn't want to look. And Molly and I didn't talk the whole way. Not a word until we got onto the elevator.

"You should probably take a bath," she said, "before Mom and Dad come home."

She was right. I hadn't taken a bath since they'd left, and my hair was still wet. My socks were wet. I just didn't want to, though. The tub was

clean, the curtains had been laundered, but still. I
went to my room and unpacked my books, but I
didn't want to do my homework either. I didn't
want to be in my room, or near the window. I didn't
want to count my mitts, or play with my fort. It was
strange. I felt as if everything I usually liked to do –
everything that was mine – had been taken from me
somehow, or contaminated.

I'd opened my math book and just, very
glumly, started my homework when a knock came
at the door, and the familiar clink of Mrs.
Guildenweiser's bracelets.

"Yes?"

She and Lara entered, though Lara didn't seem
quite as sensitive to my mood, nosing around my
baskets.

"Did you have a good day at school?" asked
Mrs. Guildenweiser.

I nodded. I didn't want to talk about the
snoring underneath the bridge.

"Is something wrong?" she asked.

I shrugged.

"Your parents are coming home tomorrow. Tomorrow night they will be here."

I nodded, I knew, and I knew that she was trying to cheer me up, but I wasn't really looking forward to my parents' coming home the way I felt I should have, because I still didn't know if I could tell them about the Beastie, and if I couldn't tell them that, what else was there to say? What was the point of saying anything?

Mrs. Guildenweiser seemed to understand. "I think I know what you might need," she said. She started fishing in her sweater pockets. "The girl called to remind – Claire – and I think it might be just the time."

She produced two white envelopes. I knew right away they were from my mother's desk. They had her handwriting on them. One had my name on it; the other, Molly's.

I opened mine right away. There was a note inside, also in my mother's handwriting:

BEASTIE

Good for one (1) soldier,
to be purchased from
Mr. Di Francini's soldier shop
during the week 4/15 - 4/20.

Mrs. Guildenweiser had figured right. We all went out together, Molly too. Her voucher was for Miss O'Neal's, which sold necklaces and bracelets and baubles and Christmas ornaments. She said she wanted to go alone, so we split up on the corner – Molly headed two blocks up; Mrs. Guildenweiser, Lara, and I, one block down.

Mr. Di Francini's soldier shop was probably my favorite store in the neighborhood, except for Rappaport's, which is where I got my mitts. I liked to go to the soldier shop at least once every couple of weeks because Mr. Di Francini was always switching things around and adding to his collection. He sold soldiers mostly – statues, too – but soldiers seemed to be his top priority, and only those of the highest quality. He would never sell the plastic molded kind. Mr. Di Francini's were heavier, made of lead and pewter, and they were planted on sturdy metal bases, and hand-painted. I had three – a knight on horseback and two Civil War infantry-men (as well as a cannon) – which stood among the rest of my soldiers like jewels among stones.

"We've come to make a purchase!" Mrs. Guildenweiser announced, as the door rattled its familiar clang and jingle behind us.

Mr. Di Francini only glanced up from behind the counter, then returned to his book, typically. Mr. Di Francini had a quiet manner about him – secretive almost, but also very agreeable. He had a large bald forehead, and an equally large round chin, which made his head the shape of a giant peanut. He wore vests, said little, and stayed behind his counter most of the time, either touching up a soldier with pencil-thin brushes, or leafing through giant collectors' books. He really only made eye contact when you actually bought something, which I didn't mind, because it meant you never felt rushed at Mr. Di Francini's. You hardly felt noticed.

BEASTIE

The space wasn't big, about the size of my parents' room, with another room in back behind a curtained door. In the center was always the largest display. Today was still the whaling boat, smashing against the bronze wave, and a harpooner standing, ready to throw. I didn't tempt myself. I kept to the walls, which were lined all the way round with glass cases, housing regiment after regiment of soldiers, each one standing tall as my hand, and hoping to be chosen. I already had an idea which piece I wanted, but I started my survey on the right-hand side, as usual, while Mrs. Guildenweiser and Lara went up to the counter to present my mother's voucher and discuss terms.

The first case was filled entirely with knights in armor, knights on horseback, knights with plumed helmets and working visors and chainmail vests and flags with griffins. There was a small catapult as well, and a turret. The next case over was all French foreign legion, with their kerchiefs on their caps (though I was never sure what they were fighting

for, defending forts in the middle of the desert).
Then there were Arabs, and Arabian horses, and
camels; then revolutionary soldiers, French and
American, redcoats, and Indians, and militia men.
There were World War I soldiers, and World War
II, some down on their stomach and crawling, some
kneeling, some charging. There were heavy tanks
and planes as well. But my personal favorite were
the Civil War soldiers. Mr. Di Francini had
hundreds – evenly split between the blues and the
grays – infantrymen and cavalry, officers, Generals,
as well as several tents and cannons. I would have
taken any of them happily, but there was one in
particular just beyond a regiment of Zouaves: a
Union Trooper on his horse. I'd had my eye on it
for a while now. He wore a blue double-breasted
shirt with gold buttons, a gold neckerchief, two
chevrons and a small-visored cap. He had a very
thick mustache, and his eyes were trained on the
horizon in a squint. His pants were grey, boots
black. He had a sword sheath, a pistol, a tobacco

pouch. His horse was in full gallop, tail whipping behind him like a flag.

"Is that your choice?" came Mr. Di Francini's voice, as always in a much kinder and calmer tone than I expected. I nodded, and he started over, pulling a key from the reel on his belt. He unlocked the glass case and slid the pane to the side.

"The Trooper, yes?"

Yes, I nodded.

Mr. Di Francini didn't seem to approve or disapprove, which made sense. He took it back to his counter, and I followed, while Mrs. Guilden-weiser discretely returned to the front of the store and took a seat by the door.

Mr. Di Francini dusted the Trooper with a flannel cloth and took a moment to examine it for chips or chinks. I didn't see any, but Mr. Di Francini seemed concerned by something. Finally, he set the Trooper down and leaned across the counter, his great head looming over me like a parade balloon. He kept his voice low.

"Now Mrs. Guildenweiser tells me you may have had an unexpected visitor."

I looked back over at her. I hadn't thought this sort of thing was allowed, but Mr. Di Francini clearly seemed to know.

I nodded.

"And why do you think this?"

"The tub," I said. "And I think he took something."

"What? If I may ask."

I was a little embarrassed to say – "A baseball mitt"– but Mr. Di Francini's reaction was very reassuring. He pressed his lips together and nodded knowingly.

"And you're afraid he might have come back?"

Not afraid, said my expression.

"But you suspect?"

"Maybe," I said. "I don't know."

Mr. Di Francini gathered the problem. He took its measure, then turned his attention back to the Union Trooper, his brows severely arched with doubt.

"I'm just not sure that's going to be big enough."

He thought for a moment, then lifted his finger to keep me in place while he ducked behind the curtain to his storage room.

I wasn't going anywhere. I looked back at Mrs. Guildenweiser, who was still in her chair by the door, Lara beside her, thumping her tail on the floor and steaming the glass with her nose. Mrs. Guildenweiser seemed to be in no hurry either. She smiled back at me and gave a faint wave.

And now Mr. Di Francini was back. "Here we are," he stepped through the curtains, but with something in his hands that I, in my wildest dreams, could never have imagined. It was the Union Trooper – exactly the same as the one I had chosen from the display case – only it was all bronze, and twice as big. Maybe three times. Maybe four.

Mr. Di Francini set it down on the counter – gently, but with an unavoidable thunk. "This is more likely to do the trick." He flicked on the desk lamp and all the details leapt at us in polished bronze – the tangles in the horse's main, the crossed swords on the cap, the wrinkles in the gloves and boots. Even the spurs had a design on them.

But I didn't understand. This was clearly a statue, not a toy. Was Mr. Di Francini offering it to me? Again I looked back at Mrs. Guildenweiser, who was just now coming over to see for herself.

"Oh, yes," she said. "That's very nice."

"Yes," said Mr. Di Francini. "Yes, it is."

"But I don't think my mother would let me," I said.

Mrs. Guildenweiser paused, not seeing why

not. She referred to the voucher, which was still right there on the counter. She spun it around to read, and turned it back to Mr. Di Francini, who likewise, once he'd put on his glasses, seemed to see no problem.

He looked down at me. "Now, do you have a window in your room?"

Yes, I nodded.

"Does it look out over the Park?"

I nodded again.

"You need to stand him in the window – at night. You can do as you like with him during the day, but at night, the window sill. Make sure there's enough space and that the view is clear. Then if the Beastie shows, he'll let you know." He tapped the Trooper's shoulder with complete confidence.

I still didn't quite understand.

"The statues," Mr. Di Francini explained. "They're the only ones that he lets see him." Mr. Di Francini gave a glance around at all the largest pieces in his collection: the harpooner in the middle of the room, the Indian in the corner, the cowboy on the bucking pony. Then he looked back at the Trooper.

"This one here should more than do."

Mrs. Guildenweiser agreed.

"So would you like a bag?" he asked.

I nodded, as that seemed to be the recommendation. Mr. Di Francini wrapped it up right there in front of me, careful to protect the most fragile parts. He wound the horse's nose and bridle in newspaper and cotton. He did the same for its tail and the Trooper's head. Then he put him in a box, which he put in a brown paper shopping bag with straps as tall as my hip.

"Good luck, then." Mr. Di Francini offered a respectful tilt of the head, and the three of us left his shop with another clang and a jingle – Lara first, then Mrs. Guildenweiser, then me with the shopping bag. I had to use two hands and hunch my shoulders just to keep the bottom from scraping the sidewalk.

BEASTIE

§

Molly wasn't pleased when she saw the size of my purchase. We met at the awning.

"What is *that*?" she asked.

"A trooper."

"The whole thing?" She looked inside the bag and saw the box. "Mom isn't going to let you keep that."

Tsk, tsk, tsk, clucked Mrs. Guildenweiser. "What did you get for yourself?"

Molly lifted her arm to show the charm bracelet on her wrist. "The shoes," she said. There was a dangling pair of tiny silver shoes. "That isn't fair. That isn't fair that you get that."

It wasn't fair, I had to agree, but I didn't feel like I'd had much say in the matter.

When we got upstairs and I took the Trooper out of his box, Molly wasn't any happier. I unwrapped all the newspaper and string and set it on the table in the living room. I didn't mean to show off, but that seemed to be the obvious place, and it did look very impressive, even more than in the shop. It was already the finest thing we owned.

"But it's a *statue*," said Molly. "I can't believe you bought a statue. I bet that counts as a birthday present, too. I bet it does."

Tsk, tsk, tsk, clucked Mrs. Guildenweiser, picking up the phone.

"Who are you calling?"

"Your mother and father. So you can thank them."

"I'm telling," said Molly.

I was, I have to admit, seized by a mild panic at this, the idea of having to explain to my mother so soon. Mrs. Guildenweiser was having trouble dialing, though, which gave me time to think. What would I say? I couldn't tell her the truth – about the Beastie, that is – not over the phone.

Mrs. Guildenweiser was taking so long that Molly finally stepped in and dialed for her. Then we all waited. Mrs. Guildenweiser spoke to someone in

French and we waited some more. The only thing that gave me any hope was the glint in Mrs. Guildenweiser eye, which was always kind of there. I had faith that she would find a way to smooth it somehow, whatever needed explaining. Then she started speaking French again, and I felt a cool wave of relief. My parents weren't there, I could tell.

"Well, we'll have to wait," she put the receiver back on the hook. "You can thank them both tomorrow."

Yes, tomorrow, I thought. Maybe by then I'd have figured out what to say.

Molly and I watched TV for two whole hours that night after dinner – all Molly's shows, but she was still angry about the statue.

"Just because you act like a big baby."

Then came bedtime. I still hadn't put the Trooper in its proper place yet – its night place. I waited for Molly to close her door before I went to get it from the living room. I had to carry it with two hands.

Mrs. Guildenweiser caught me just as I was sneaking back into my room. She followed me. Lara too, trotting and sniffing and smacking her tail against the radiator.

"You shouldn't mind your sister," said Mrs. Guildenweiser. She watched as I set the Trooper on the windowsill, just as Mr. Di Francini said. She helped clear away what was there, some pens and crayons and paperclips, and she lifted the shade to make sure the view was clear. "Your mother will like him. He's very beautiful, don't you think?"

I wasn't sure that 'beautiful' was the word I'd use, but I had to agree. Definitely the Trooper was one of the most *handsome* things I'd ever seen. How one could not be happy to have it in their home – unless they were jealous like Molly – I couldn't imagine, especially the way it looked right now: the bronze of the Trooper's outward-facing features lit gold by the street lamp, and casting a crooked blue shadow against the casement. I was seriously considering never asking for anything again.

Mrs. Guildenweiser said good night then. She gave the Trooper's horse one last pat on the rump. Lara offered a few final sniffs, and they left us alone.

I propped up my pillow up against the headboard to get a good view, so that whenever I opened my eyes, the Trooper would be the first thing I saw. I tested several times – closing and opening, closing and opening – and every time, the Trooper was right there where he should be, standing guard, he and his beaming blue profile slanted against the frame: the crook in his nose, the brim of his hat, the knot of the kerchief around his neck . . .

Chapter Five:
the turtle pond

. . . And I wouldn't have said I fell asleep. I would have said I was on the *verge* of falling asleep when I heard the familiar sound of the front door clicking shut. I sat straight up. Were Mom and Dad home already? But it was still dark. I listened, but there was no more sound. I turned. I crept out of bed even, to peak into the hallway. Lara was asleep on her side like a rug. The front door, still. I turned back to my room and suddenly my breath caught in my throat: The window shade was flat against the sash. The Trooper wasn't there.

Then I saw there was a tennis ball on the floor, ever so infinitesimally rocking back and forth in

the evening breeze. The closet door was open.

I got down on my knees and very slowly I crawled over to where I could see, knee by knee, but there was no one in the closet. Just the shorter of the two baskets, tipped on its side and empty, all but for some stray pucks and balls huddled together. The mitts, gone.

And now there was a sound outside the window. *Clip-clop clip-clop clip-clop.* I went to the sill and looked down just in time to see the Trooper crossing the street. It was very clearly him, even though he seemed to be life-size now. He was still bronze, and he had his sword and his pistol, and he was just now stepping the pony up onto the sidewalk where the hot dog man stood his wagon during the day. The only difference, aside from his size, was that he also had a sack slung over his right shoulder, full like a laundry bag but much chunkier. And now he was entering the park with it. My baseball mitts.

I ran. I put on my slippers and went as fast as I could. I had to tiptoe over Lara and make sure the front door didn't creak too loud, but as soon as I was out in the hall, I raced. I took the stairs so as not to rouse the elevator man, down six smooth bannisters and past the snoring doorman. I ran across the sleeping street with all the sleeping cars, and knowing if my mother saw, she would have had a heart attack, I did the one thing I was most supposed not to do. In the middle of the night, and wearing nothing but my pajamas and slippers, I entered the park.

By the light of the lamp post up ahead, I caught a glimpse of the pony's tail just now turning right onto the first bridge. The Trooper was headed for the museum and the playing fields.

I kept running, with shadows trailing me and leading me, and twisting all around me. By the time I made it across the bridge, the Trooper was entering the underpass up ahead, the one where we'd all taken shelter from the rain. I could hear the pony's hooves chattering against the arched brick. I kept running – past the museum and into the shadow as fast as I could, through the echo of my scuffing slippers.

But then when I came out the other side, I heard giggling, clearly. The Trooper was still up ahead, nearing the bank of the turtle pond, and he still had the sack over his shoulder. I had to catch him, but now a voice called out from behind.

"Pssssst!..Pssssst!"

I stopped. It was coming from the giant stone needle.

"Who is that there?"

It was a girl's voice, with an English accent, but with the lamp post behind her and the trees all black and leafy, all I could see was her outline: her long flowing hair, the little bow on top, the puffs at the shoulder of her dress, and the way it ballooned out from her waist like an umbrella. I knew who it was. There was her slender polished finger, pointing out at me.

"Who are you?" she asked.

The others from the toadstool were there as

well. The rabbit in the dress coat, and the buck-toothed dwarf in the top hat and giant bow tie. Even the cat was stretched out on the limb above the others, swinging its bronze tail like a feather.

"What are you doing here?" she asked. "I don't think you're supposed to be."

"No room, no room," teased the buck-toothed man with a wave of his hand.

"Well, of course there's room," said the girl, but…" She peered closer at me, as if *I* were the strange looking one, all flesh and bone and pajamas and hair. "Who let you in?"

All of a sudden I wasn't sure. I looked to the Trooper, who'd stopped not far ahead, beneath another glowing lamp post.

"He took my mitts."

The Trooper looked back at us quietly, now pinching a black clump from his bronze tobacco pouch and stuffing it under his giant mustache. He didn't deny.

"But it's so warm?" said the girl, confused.

"Who needs mitts?"

"Baseball mitts." I pointed back at the sack hanging over the Trooper's shoulder.

"My, my," clucked the buck-toothed man. "How many mitts do you have?"

I thought. Nine minus the catcher's mitt. "Eight."

"Eight? How many hands do you have?"

"Two."

"Then shouldn't two mitts do?"

Clearly he knew nothing about baseball, but he had a good point just the same.

"But they're still mine," I said.

"They're whosever-they-are's," said the dwarf off-handedly, "but do what you like."

I wasn't sure what that was yet. I looked to the Trooper, who looked back at me and for the first time he spoke, his voice low and even, and slightly muffled by the combination of his mustache and all the tobacco in his mouth.

"I thought you'd want to see him."

I didn't have to ask whom he was talking about. We all knew.

"Do you?" asked the girl. "Is that really what you're doing here?"

I still wasn't sure, but over to the right, a crackling of twigs and fallen buds announced the presence of another group of heavy shadows stepping out from under the trees. It was the story teller – he still had the giant book in his hand – and the Polish king was with him, Jaggiello (pronounced Ya-yellow), though he had dismounted. The great horse was behind them in its cape, drinking at the edge of the pond, but I recognized the King by his scowl, by his fish-scale breastplate and his two heavy swords.

And there was the duckling as well now, waddling up to see what all the fuss was about.

I was definitely most impressed by the story-teller, maybe because he was so tall, standing up. I couldn't see his face beneath the canopy of leaves, except for the patch of lamplight on his long nose. He had the book with him. I only knew two of the stories inside – the one about the duckling, and the one about the boy and the Emperor who wasn't wearing any clothes – but I realized it probably wasn't a good idea trying to lie in front of the man who made that up. Or his statue. So I turned to the Trooper and nodded, yes, that's why I was here – to see the Beastie – because that was the truth.

With that, the Trooper swung the sack around from his shoulder. He tipped it upside down and out spilled all the baseball gloves, tumbling onto the grass and taking a moment to settle. I counted all eight, including my gamer.

"Shouldn't take too long," the Trooper murmured.

Just then the Rabbit's ears flicked to the north side of the field. "Shshsh," said the girl, and we all turned as at that moment a distant howl sounded. The Cheshire Cat jumped down from its limb and started pacing behind the girl. Jaggiello lifted his head. *There he is*, he seemed to be saying, but I couldn't see so far away and in the dark – just a

rustling in the leaves of a distant tree all the way on
the far side of the field.

But then it seemed to move, the rustling did, to
the next tree over, and then the next, like a tight
little breeze coming this way. We could see the
progress very clearly now, all the limbs and leaves
bowing beneath the weight, shivering in his
presence, and nodding in his wake. Another
moment and he'd come all the way around. A

shadow fell from the nearest limb and tumbled forward up onto a bench, then up onto the cap of the lamp post just like that, so perfectly balanced and still, it was as if he'd been perching there the whole time.

He wasn't very big, but with the lamplight underneath him it was hard to make out more – just a dark low figure, with pointed ears on top of his head, and a low, swinging arm.

The Trooper stepped his horse back from the mitts to clear the way, and in another blink the Beastie jumped down and tumbled to an upright stop in front of us. I could see him much better now. He really wasn't very tall – not so much taller than me, but he was shaped almost like a fire hydrant with legs. He was covered from head to toe in a dark thick coat of hair, though less so around his calves and feet, which were very large. He had a small pot-belly beneath his fur, upon which rested an extra abundance of hair trailing from his chin like a beard. He had a very large mouth, with an equally broad flat forehead. His eyes were buried deep beneath his brow, but I could still see them peering out – two faint glimmers of light, just bright enough to show…how familiar he seemed. His appearance was in no way surprising to me, but surprisingly familiar.

The mitts were all still there at his very hairy (but very human-seeming) feet. He picked one up, my gamer. He sniffed it and his eyes rolled back in ecstasy. I knew exactly what he wanted to do, but he didn't for some reason. Instead he picked up a second mitt, the first baseman's. He twisted it backwards, stared at it thoughtfully for a moment, then stuffed the whole thing into his mouth like a giant dumpling. I didn't budge. I stood and watched as the Beastie chewed the mitt slowly with a great rolling jaw, and as he did, his deep dark eyes slid over beneath his brow. He looked directly at me, grinning, and swallowed with an open gulp. I could hear the mitt sliding down his throat and landing softly in his belly. His stomach offered a low rumble of contentment.

"You're welcome," I said, finally realizing what it was that wasn't true about the Beastie: not that he existed − he clearly did − but that there was anything remotely frightening about him.

The Beastie glanced around now. He hadn't known so many were there − Alice and her friends, the storyteller, the duckling, and the Polish King. He didn't seem bothered, though. He took his time. He picked up a third glove − he still had the gamer tucked beneath his arm − but now he took a sniff of the raggedy outfielder's glove and slid it back inside the Trooper's sack. He did the same with the pitcher's mitt, the one with all the tar, then all the rest from seasons gone by. He gathered them up like vegetables and stuffed them in the duffel.

The only one remaining now was my gamer. He held it in his giant, hairy, knuckly hand. I wouldn't have blamed him if he'd eaten it right there, it looked so delicious. But again he didn't. He dropped it back on the grass where he'd found it.

He was leaving it there.

He took up the sack now, heavy with mitts, swung it over his shoulder, and started off across the path, tumbling once or twice and offering little humming grunts as his goodbye. He split between the storyteller and the duck, and started around the Turtle Pond, past Jaggiello's horse. There weren't so many trees that way, so he rolled and hopped and tumbled along the bank, all the way out onto the rocks beneath the Castle. Then he scrambled up

and slipped inside the lowest window, a black sliver in the stone.

I thought, so that was where he slept all day, and snored for everyone to hear.

"You should go," whispered Alice from behind.

The Trooper agreed. "Sun'll be up soon. They have to head back."

The rabbit in the dress coat consulted his pocket watch and nodded, it was true.

"I need to wash my hands," said the buck-toothed man.

"And I still have to find my ribbon," said the girl.

Oh, yes, oh, yes, all agreed, with a perceptible droop in their shoulders. I grabbed my one remaining mitt – my gamer – and the Trooper lifted me up onto the pony. I'd never felt so light, like a feather on his arm. I sat up front, holding onto the horse's mane for balance. The statues all raised their hands in farewell. The Polish King Jaggiello crossed his swords above his head.

With that, the Trooper tapped his heels and started us away — down the path and through the little tunnel, then past the museum on the left. At least I assume that's the way he went, though I have to admit that all the excitement was finally catching up with me, and that the lateness of the hour, combined with the gentle sway of the pony's stride and the warmth of his saddle, sent me off to a deep and very peaceful sleep long before we ever reached the street again.

epilogue

My parents returned the following day, as scheduled. They were there when Molly and I got home from school. They both looked very happy – happy from their time away, and happy to be back. Their hugs and kisses were extra long and hard, and made me realize how much I had missed them. I'd been so preoccupied, I hadn't noticed.

We ate dinner together in the dining room. Mrs. Guildenweiser joined us as well, as thanks, and Lara. We ordered Chinese, and told about everything we'd missed. My parents described the places they'd seen. There *had* been bicycles, in fact, and a beach, but it was still hard to picture, without us there. Molly talked about school mostly, and her friends, and when it was my turn I told them how my coach had put me at shortstop. I told them about the Blue Team Fight Song, and the Trojan Horse, and how one of the seventh graders got his left nostril torn off in an eraser fight (or torn "loose," as Molly pointed out). I had to explain about the Trooper as well. My mother had noticed it the moment they got home, out on the table in the living room, so I told them what was true, which was that I hadn't meant to get anything so big, but that Mr. Di Francini had insisted. Mrs. Guilden-weiser confirmed the story, and luckily my parents agreed with me about how handsome the Trooper was. Unless you were Molly, you couldn't very well look at it and wish it weren't there, and even she didn't seem so bothered by it anymore.

But the one thing I did not tell my parents about was the Beastie. Not even after dinner when they came in to say good night. I hid my baskets in the closet so they wouldn't see my mitts were gone, and I let the Trooper spend the evening in the living room. Again they kissed me and told me how much they had missed me. They said that next time maybe they'd bring me and Molly with them, and I said I'd like that too, but I still didn't mention anything about what had *really* happened that week.

BEASTIE

I wasn't sure why, except that it didn't feel like I was lying to them. If my parents didn't already know about Beastie – and who was to say, maybe they did; you can never be sure about such things – but if they didn't, then I figured they'd find out when they were good and ready, just as Mrs. Guildenweiser said.

Which still leaves the question of why I'm telling you all this, and whether that means you're ready – just for having read. And there I think the answer may come back to what Mr. Ryan said, which is that no matter what I've told you here, it's still your job figure out which parts are true and which parts aren't. And maybe you'll know, or maybe you won't. Either way, I'd say the secret's safe, and that's the most important thing. That's what's best for everyone, I think.

Best for Beastie, too.